I0788152

LUMPY THE DOLPHIN AND THESE SAVAGE SEAS

Alan Cooper

Alan Cooper

Dedication

To all the dolphins – victims of human violence in the fishing industry and the captivity industry, to dolphins like Lumpy. To all the great leviathans like Mr. Sperm, victims of the whaling industry. When they are all gone, man will die from a great loneliness of spirit.

Acknowledgement

To capitalism and greedy people for making me aware that money is just paper and valueless unless used wisely. That people and animals are more important than gold, as is this precious, lonely, inhabited globe spinning through the cosmos.

Alan Cooper

Table of Contents

About the Author

Alan Cooper, a Manchester-born activist, has been a dedicated vegan for 42 years and has a long history within the animal rights movement. During the 1980s and 1990s, he was deeply involved in direct action campaigns, serving an eight-month prison sentence for burglary and conspiracy related to the liberation of animals from a testing laboratory.

Alan spent over two decades campaigning to close dolphinariums in the UK, successfully targeting establishments such as Morecambe and Flamingo Land. Flamingo Land officially closed on March 8, 1993, marking the end of dolphinarium openings in the country. Following these victories, he extended his activism internationally, collaborating with campaigners in Sweden, Belgium, Finland, and other countries to support local animal rights efforts.

In the late 1990s, Alan moved from his native Manchester to Dorset. While he appreciates the reduced risk of burglaries in his new home, he still misses the Saddleworth Moors, where he spent many happy days bog-trotting with his faithful dog, Champ. Now living alone, Alan shares his house with more unconventional animal companions, including woodlice and moths.

For more information, visit
www.dolphin-lover.me.uk

Alan Cooper

The Amble Legend

A wild dolphin the author spent hundreds of hours swimming with.

Touched by a dolphin

A grey torpedo approaches

Grinning

Primed to explode

A quarter ton blubber bully boy sometimes

Sometimes

Looking at you, looking at me

Through that deep brown eye

I wonder what are your dreams?

A knowing eye filled with joy and wildness

A touch of dolphin rubs me,

If only for a while

- Alan Cooper

Alan Cooper

Lumpy's Birth

Lumpy's mother was overjoyed. "Isn't she beautiful?" she said to the other two dolphins who were present at the birth.

Much like human midwives, they were there just in case of any complications. Unlike human births, this calf emerged tail-first to prevent the risk of drowning during a slow delivery. These dolphins were conscious breathers, unlike humans, who breathe without a second thought.

"Yes, she is a beauty," the mid-dolphins agreed, their faces blushing with admiration. It wasn't the right moment to mention that the newborn had an odd-shaped tail, a slight disability, and some peculiar markings or lumps on her otherwise smooth skin. As the calf emerged, she was gently guided to the surface for her very first breath on the Blue Planet and quickly reunited with her mother.

Grumpy, or Mum, was even more delighted to know that it was a girl, for she held values that humans might label as feminist.

Lumpy, as a young calf, never ventured far from her mother for protection and nourishment. They swam close to the surface since Lumpy needed to breathe more frequently at the water's edge.

One day, they encountered strong currents and large waves, making it difficult for Lumpy to both swim and breathe. "I don't like this, Mum," she cried out. "I just swallowed water, Mum!" Grumpy responded, "My dear, as

I told you before, blow out first to clear the water from your nostrils or blowhole before inhaling only air.”

To any observer, the scene would have seemed quite amusing – a dolphin, the epitome of grace, experiencing an ungraceful moment. As time passed, Lumpy grew rapidly thanks to her mother’s nourishing milk. One day, as they were swimming, a massive shape loomed before them, startling Lumpy.

“What’s that?” she asked.

“Hello, you are quite big, Mr. Whale,” Grumpy greeted the newcomer.

“Hello! Little dolphins, but please address me properly. I am a Sperm whale,” the massive creature responded in a deep and intense voice.

Lumpy, ever curious, inquired, “Why are you called that?” Even Grumpy couldn’t help but smile at her daughter’s question.

“I don’t know, but the two-legged, troublesome human ones have a name for all of us. They named one of my cousins the ’Right Whale’ because it would float instead of sinking when killed. Sperm whales are deep thinkers. We have the biggest brains in this ocean and on the planet. Around 4 kgs compared to the two-legged ones, half the size of ours!” he said with a hint of annoyance in his voice.“I must go, dolphins. I don’t like you a lot,” Mr. Sperm Whale grumbled, his frustration evident. “You zoom around over me, under me, buzz me with your chattering nonsense, call me a big head, square head, and some days I think if I ever grab one, I'll swallow it whole. All you lot want to do is muck about in play and enjoy life. We whales are deep thinkers, trying to plan ways we can combat the destruction humans create. I have an important meeting to attend."

Grumpy offered an apology with a weary smile, acknowledging, "It will be because boys will be boys," a phrase often used to excuse male foolishness.

Most of the males, particularly the adolescents, bored Lumpy. *Look at me, how fast I swim, how deep I dive, how high I jump acrobatically — BORING!* she would yell, using the dolphin equivalent: a series of echolocation clicks.

These clicks were sent out to an object, and the returning signal provided a precise image, revealing the object's shape, size, and distance.

Males typically took charge of decisions related to hunting, playing, relaxing, and napping. The state of the tide and the currents largely dictated their movements and choices.

"But, why couldn't consensus make decisions?" she wondered. "I prefer it when we are other females. Lumpy, rather than in a mixed pod, we sometimes mix in, and the adolescents in their pod stay well away from us."

As Lumpy continued to grow, she had opportunities to explore the coastal waters, where she encountered various marine life. She marvelled at crabs scuttling along the sea bottom and the colourful fish that darted about. She cherished the way sunlight filtered through the water, creating enchanting patterns of dancing rays. One day, she noticed a group of dolphins that were different from their usual companions, the bottlenose dolphins. Curiosity got the better of her, and she swam closer to them, extending a friendly greeting.

Grumpy's voice carried with concern, "Come back here! You are not to play with those; they are a different species – common dolphins."

She was also a bit of a snob! By now, Lumpy was acutely aware of her differences. Other dolphins made fun of her, hurling insults, and both males and females teased her with names like 'slowcoach Lumpy' and worse.

Lumpy's inquisitiveness and sensitivity led her to ask, "Mum, why are other dolphins so cruel to me?" Her mother felt a wave of sadness for her daughter and offered comforting words, "Daughter, let it wash over you like a wave; don't let their name-calling affect you. They tease you because they are unhappy in their own lives; you are a beautiful individual, my precious daughter."

As Grumpy consoled her, a tear welled up in Lumpy's eye, and she continued, "There's something else that bothers me. Can you tell me why we need to eat fish? Why do we need to kill?"

Grumpy smiled at her daughter's compassion and gently replied, "Well, my dear, we do it to survive; dolphins have always done that."

Lumpy's tears flowed freely now, and she sniffled as she continued, "But Mum, just because it's always been done, does that make it right?"

Grumpy had no easy answer to provide.

Grumpy Is Captured

The day that forever changed their lives began like any other, with the pair swimming not far from the shoreline, observing the two-legged creatures frolicking on the beach.

"Mum," Lumpy questioned, "Mr. Sperm Whale said they were evil, but they don't look evil to me."

Grumpy, unknowingly foreshadowing the future, responded, "Some may not be, dear."

Suddenly, their tranquillity was shattered by the high-pitched noise of two speeding boats racing towards them. Before they could escape, a net encircled them, tightened, and lifted them out of the water, depositing them on the deck of one of the boats.

"Got you, my beauties!" one man shouted triumphantly.

Another said, "One of them seems to have an odd-shaped tail and marks on her skin. We can't sell her. You know they want perfect-looking ones for the shows."

"Throw her back," said the first man, hesitating.

The second man retorted, "Put them both back? They look like mother and adolescent."

"What, and lose thousands of dollars? Don't be a sentimental fool."

In a matter of minutes, Lumpy met humans for the first time and lost her mother.

Though Lumpy couldn't comprehend the full significance of the men's remarks, Grumpy had once explained that toxic chemicals might have caused the lumps and marks on her skin in the seas. PCBs, or polychlorinated biphenyl, were used in electrical equipment. If these chemicals seeped into rivers and estuaries, they became insoluble in water. Through the food chain, these toxins found their way into the blubber or fat of dolphins like Lumpy, or they were passed from mother to calf through the milk. Post-mortems in Cardigan Bay recorded nearly 300 parts per million in a baby dolphin, a level well above human legal limits, which considered only a few parts per million as acceptable. In the St. Lawrence River in Canada, the Beluga white whales were regarded as toxic waste when found dead.

Back in the water, Lumpy screamed and screamed, "MUM! MUM! MUM!" Her cries echoed through the water, and within minutes, other dolphins arrived to comfort her.

"What happened?" they inquired.

Lumpy explained the distressing encounter with the humans, and the group solemnly nodded, recounting similar experiences where pod members disappeared. "We never saw them again. There was Betty, Lotty, Sharky, Lady, and Rocky, but we never saw or heard from them again. You will never see Grumpy again," they coldly reiterated.

But Lumpy was determined, and she screamed back, "I WILL! I WILL! I WILL! I will find Mr. Whale and ask for his help."

With the passage of several tides and moons, she eventually found Mr. Sperm Whale and shared her plight with him.

He expressed his sorrow and assured her, "I can send out messages to other whales, and we'll see what can be done and what information we can gather. Our echolocation can travel for hundreds of miles, and, as you know, water is far better than air at transmitting sound. Someone will have heard or seen something."

Unbeknownst to them, the intelligence and compassion of a few humans would soon intersect with their struggle. Outside Marineland, animal rights activists were protesting the captivity of dolphins.

"Have you heard this nonsense?" one activist remarked.

"Yes, it's almost comical, but it's heartbreaking to confine a dolphin in a bare concrete box," another replied.

They were members of a group known as the Morecambe Dolphin Campaign.They had heard media reports that Rocky had a new companion, and the tabloids reported it was "love at first sight." Their information had likely been fed to them by dolphinaria apologists, possibly from Flamingo Land in Yorkshire, one of the four dolphin shows left in the UK.

The decline in the number of such shows over the decades was largely due to the regular deaths of dolphins, which were challenging and costly to replace. The public was also becoming more discerning as they became aware of the plight of these magnificent creatures, thanks to human campaigners who stood outside the dolphin shows with educational flyers and banners proclaiming messages like "Don't see me, free me" and "Born free, swim free, captivity kills."

The lives of Lumpy and Grumpy were about to take an unexpected turn as the voice of compassion began to reach far and wide, resonating with others who cared deeply for the well-being of these magnificent creatures.

Adam chimed in, "How could they have approved it and issued an import license?"

Russell explained, "To import a dolphin into the EU, it needs to be for education, breeding, or scientific research." He continued with a hint of frustration, "Hey presto, they can meet any of those EU conditions."

The group discussed the situation further, including the dolphins' well-being, the potential aggression between them, and whether they were truly happy.

"I hear they have even given her the name 'Happy.' We need to get someone they don't recognise to get good photos with identifying marks. We need to find out if they are getting on okay or if there is any aggression, rake marks from teeth on bodies, or jaw snapping at one another. We need to see if she really is happy, and If my name isn't extremely grumpy," Adam declared, "we'll get Happy out and return her to where she belongs – the blue of the ocean."

They also saw an opportunity to free Rocky in the process, believing that this so-called "love at first sight" was, in human terms, "a forced marriage."

***

Later, Lumpy returned to Mr. Sperm for updates. "I didn't hear anything for a few days," she said, but then he relayed important information.

"Bingo," he said cryptically.

"What is bingo?" inquired Lumpy.

"Never mind," Mr. Sperm replied, "but it means I can tell you this: a boat with a dolphin onboard was seen leaving the Mediterranean Sea, travelling into the Atlantic Ocean, and heading north into the Irish Sea. The boat disembarked the dolphin at a place known as Morecambe Marineland, an old and run-down dolphinarium not far from the sea."

Mr. Sperm shared that his whale friends had heard distressed cries from a lone male dolphin named Rocky. There were suspicions that the humans wanted a female companion for him, possibly to breed, which could attract visitors and boost profits. It seemed that Grumpy may have been sold to this place.

Lumpy's determination was unwavering as she stated, "I must go and find my Mum. Will you help me, Mr. Sperm?"

After a thoughtful pause, he agreed to assist, offering to carry her on his back for a quicker journey. "It will cost you ten SQUIDS," he playfully added, a reference to their upcoming squid hunt.

"Before we leave, I suggest we eat lunch. I must dive deep to find those squid – messy but tasty creatures, those cephalopods." A short time later, he said, "That filled my tummy for a while, yummy, yummy."

As soon as he said that, he spewed up and said with a sigh, "I get called big head. Sometimes, amongst all the waste humans dump in the oceans, I like to recycle. But most of the plastic cartons and fishing nets are a hazard and a symptom of a human society that isn't functioning correctly – one that just doesn't care, an out-of-sight, out-of-mind way of thinking. But we have to live and sometimes die with their waste."

"There is," he continued, "a cousin of yours called the Indus dolphin. It sometimes carries the young on its back and also swims sideways with just one flipper or pectoral fin, using the other to disturb creatures at the sea bottom. Very sad, but there are only around 1000 left alive now in the Indus River in Pakistan."

A loud noise brought something up. "Let's go, hop on board," he commanded Lumpy.

She settled awkwardly. "How will this work, Mr. Sperm?"

"It will work fine in relation to Einstein's theories of relativity and motion."

"What?" came the reply.

"Yes, it was a book I picked up on the ocean floor – a fascinating read. I understood it in thirty minutes. I suppose it's why I am called big head."

Lumpy, however, couldn't help but question her companion's dietary habits. She asked about the small fish Mr. Sperm sometimes swallowed. He responded by discussing the complexities of their coexistence with human waste and its tragic consequences. He even shared a human fascination with a material called ambergris, highly valued for use in perfumes.

Lumpy couldn't help but comment on the whale lice clinging to Mr. Sperm. She also suggested that he clean his teeth, to which Mr. Sperm chuckled, revealing his views on humans' role in ocean pollution. Despite the humorous exchange, Lumpy had a more significant concern: the large, creepy creatures she could see on Mr. Sperm's back. Barnacles and whale lice were a regular occurrence, but she found the latter ticklish.

"Sometimes, in scorching weather," he explained, "I surface, and they congregate on the tip of my head. Then, I flick them off, and, hey presto, a tasty snack of sun-dried, fried lice."

They continued to share lighthearted moments despite the strange diet choices of cetaceans.Their progress was slow, as Mr. Sperm would have to dive to catch cephalopods, and Lumpy caught some fish. They swam close to the surface as Lumpy had to breathe air regularly. Mr. Sperm could dive very deep, 1000 meters or more, and didn't have to breathe as often.

Two amazing things happened; first, when they came up to breathe, they nearly sank a small dinghy full of humans.

"That was lucky," said Mr. Sperm, "I didn't hear the infernal noise of an engine. It does my head in that incessant throbbing and noise pollution."

The humans on board – the dinghy – were startled; to put it mildly, most of them had never seen the sea before, let alone a huge whale. They came from countries like Afghanistan, Iran, and Iraq, and they were fleeing religious persecution or economic hardship and trying to find a better life in Europe. Some called them migrants or refugees; others with empathy called them fellow humans in need of help and compassion. They usually headed for southern Italy or Malta because it was a short journey from Lebanon or Libya.

"The engine must have failed," said Mr. Sperm. "I've seen dead bodies before after that happened, young children, floating lifeless; it felt like my big heart was breaking. What drives people to leave their homeland to go to another country where they know few people, which has a different language and culture, leaving family, is called desperation; that's what Lumpy. They have no common melodic whale song or even monotonous dolphin clicks to communicate with each other, and they haven't evolved like us. We are going to help Lumpy."

And with that, he positioned his head at the back of the boat and, with such gentleness but equal force, began pushing the floating boat towards land.

Whether it was luck or deliberate, it was towards the European coastline. At first, the boat people didn't realise what was happening; then, losing their fear and apprehension, they began shouting and clapping, taking out their phones to take pictures.

One who was aware of Western capitalism shouted that we were going to be rich and famous when we told this story to the world. When they were close to land, Mr. Sperm stopped pushing and, as he did, slapped his tail fluke. The people shouted thanks as they realised they were in sight of land.

"Well done, Mr. Sperm," said Lumpy, and she jumped out of the water and into the air in celebration.

"One of the advantages of being called big head is that for a minute, I nearly stopped when one of them asked if it was a mother and baby. The cheek of calling me a female."

"I don't know why that should offend you. My Mum says females are superior to males. She says if they disagree with you, they sulk and say, I am going out for the night. My Mum says females collaborate. My Mum also says it is only females who know the pain and joy of birth and death."

"My Mum says you are giving my big head a big headache. Lumpy, quiet now."

In the distance, they could see the humans now safely on dry land; some were still waving, some were crying tears of joy, some were praying, and some were shouting Allah-hu-Akbar.

"They are saying I am great."

"Mr. Sperm, are you sure, or is it a whale of a lie!"

As they continued, they entered the Narrows or Straits of Gibraltar. They saw more and bigger boats, and the underwater noise rattled in their heads from the boat engines.

"You'll never push those," Lumpy said.

"Of course, I could," Mr. Sperm said, even though he knew he couldn't. "They don't need help, and those are whale and dolphin-watching boats. They want to see us and take photographs. Let's give them one to remember."

Lumpy rose to the surface to see tens of humans pointing their cameras at them. Snap, snap, snap went the shutters and shouts.

"I don't believe it," one said. "I have been taking photographs for years, and that looks like a bottlenose dolphin on the back and being carried by a Sperm whale. It just can't be. I have it captured by the digital camera."

"So do I," said another. "And I," said another.

"This is unknown in cetology. If what we think is happening is, cetacean experts worldwide will have to see this. They will say we have exaggerated what we have seen, but we have the proof of our eyes and cameras."

Just as they heard this, Mr. Sperm laughed so loudly he nearly shook his passenger off his back and said that he would give the scientists something to debate and argue about for the next fifty years!

***

"What, Mr. Sperm, is that? It was miles away, but the noise was intense. It must be several times your size."

"That is what humans know as a submarine, and the low-frequency sound LFS it is emitting will kill us if we don't get out of the noise range soon. I know there have been incidents of our kind beaching off the land due to the intense sound after they have become disorientated."

"A submarine; what is that?" Lumpy asked.

"They are war machines that can travel undetected. What you need to understand, Lumpy, is that humans have only existed as a species for tens of thousands of years; they are still primitive, exist in places they call countries, and are full of aggression if they disagree about," he paused.

Lumpy asked, "About?"

"About almost anything, and war is the end result in which they kill millions of humans and millions of other animals that get in the way. Let's move quickly. Get on my back," he told Lumpy, and with that, he dived deeply down.

Their journey took them from the Mediterranean Sea into the Atlantic, a much larger and less familiar body of water for Mr. Sperm.

Lumpy asked why he preferred the smaller seas, to which he replied, "I'd rather be a big whale in a small sea than a small one in a big sea."

As they swam through the Strait of Gibraltar, they encountered various other marine life, including dolphins, octopuses, and porpoises, who all had their own playful interactions with the odd couple.

As they reached the Cornish coast, the public started reporting sightings of the unique pair. News of the "odd couple" quickly spread, and people flocked to the coast to catch a glimpse, transforming the phenomenon into a kind of twitching or bird-watching for marine life enthusiasts. Mr. Sperm and Lumpy had become international celebrities, captivating the world's attention.

As they continued their journey, they navigated the Irish Sea while avoiding a ghost net—a discarded and deadly fishing net floating aimlessly in the ocean. Their adventure was drawing closer to its conclusion, and the mission to reunite Lumpy with her mother and potentially free Rocky was about to reach its climax.

He explained to Lumpy the different types of nets that humans used, which included purse seines, trawling nets, gill nets, and long lines. Long lines were unique, he told her, as they were tens of miles long, each segment baited with hooks to catch fish and potentially snare other marine life. A trawl net was typically dragged behind a boat, or sometimes two boats working in pairs, scraping the sea bottom and capable of catching anything in its path. These nets had been known to float thousands of miles with ocean currents. Gill nets, on the other hand, were designed to be buoyant but acted as invisible walls of death, often used at the surface or depth. They could become lost and float if the anchors were detached.

"Purse seines," he continued, "are nets used to target fish that can be spotted with the help of machines in the sky. For instance, when humans see pods of dolphins swimming with species like yellowfin tuna, they encircle the whole group or pod, and the net traps them all."

He explained that if a dolphin got caught in the nylon invisible net because their echolocation couldn't detect it, it would either result in gruesome injuries or a slow, drowning death. "I've seen everything," Mr. Sperm said, "crabs, lobsters, skates, rays, sharks, birds, and fish that humans are trying to catch, but they don't seem to care much about the lives they murder, the bycatch that gets caught. They call it accidental, playing with words in their human language, but the correct term is incidental, meaning a direct consequence of their actions.

"You are so wise," Lumpy said, deeply moved.

"And remember, it's only that wisdom that saved us from those fishing nets," Mr. Sperm reminded her.

***

Adam picked up Sorrel and rushed to the others at the dolphinarium entrance. "Quick, I think we have a live-stranded dolphin. Dial 999 and ask for the coastguard. After that, someone rings the media," he urged. It was 1990, and mobile phones were the size of house bricks, but they had to act swiftly. "We'll leave two people picketing here; the rest of us, let's go to the dolphin." Adam was the undoubted leader, having been to university, while the rest were less privileged but more educated and streetwise. Within a few minutes, they were by Lumpy's side.

While waiting for the arrival of the British Divers Marine Life Rescue (BDMLR) team, Adam laid out a plan. "Keep the dolphin wet to avoid overheating. Their blubber normally keeps them warm, but out of the water, it can be lethal. We need to ensure water doesn't enter the blowhole or eyes."

Everyone was nervously excited, except for Rocky and Happy, who had never seen a true wild dolphin up close.

"Can't we just lift the dolphin back?" someone asked.

"No," Adam replied firmly, "trying to lift a quarter-ton animal could risk dislocating its spine or flippers. We wait for a specially adapted stretcher with holes for the flippers, roll the dolphin onto it, and float it back. Get to the van, get all the cushions, and if needed, rip out the seats. We need to place them under the dolphin to ease the pressure on its internal organs." They didn't know that Lumpy had already experienced such handling on the capture boat.

Once the cushions were in place, they left just two people talking soothingly to Lumpy. "We don't want to crowd around and cause further stress," Adam advised. "It will be in shock and stress now."

The coastguard and BDMLR team were on their way. When they retreated, it was Sorrel who said, "Dad, I think I saw a big head poking out of the sea."

Adam was intrigued, "A big square head?"

Sorrel nodded, "Yes, Dad, a big square head!"

He gasped, realising the potential danger, "Oh my golly, golly, vegan fruit gumdrops! I hope that isn't going to strand. A sperm whale weighs tons and tons!"

But Sorrel reassured him, "I think it's okay. It seems to be hanging around as if it's waiting for something."

Suddenly, it clicked in Adam's mind. "Sperm Whale and Dolphin, IT'S THE ODD COUPLE! THEY'RE HERE ON PURPOSE!"

Lumpy could feel the touch of human hands on her body. She could hear a strange yet reassuring noise coming from their mouths.

They were saying, "We are here to take care of you and put you back in the sea. Soon, there will be more people here with special equipment to do that." Tears were falling from their eyes, and she felt a deep sense of gratitude.

Mr. Sperm kept poking his head out to see what was happening, feeling helpless. He had become fond of Lumpy, and he realised he had a better understanding of both dolphins and the female gender. He reflected on how it was usually the male dolphins who antagonised him, and he threw up some more ambergris at the thought of Lumpy being hurt or worse. His only solace was that the humans seemed to be genuinely trying to help.

The police and coastguard had alerted British Divers Marine Life Rescue (BDMLR), a group of dedicated volunteers who attended strandings around the UK. They also ran training courses for the public to prepare them for such situations. Time was critical, and the longer Lumpy lay stranded, the less her chances of survival. MDC had done their part, and now it was up to the vet and BDMLR to do theirs. They arrived within the hour, and the marine vet examined Lumpy carefully, monitoring her breathing, which seemed normal at eight breaths per minute. Fortunately, there were no signs of injuries to her body. Sometimes, in cases of severe suffering or when there was nothing more that could be done, they had to euthanise the animal to prevent further pain. But this time, the vet had good news. "We're good to go and get her back," he announced.

They rolled Lumpy very gently onto a specially adapted stretcher and waited for the incoming tide to help support her weight. They turned her to face the sea, and slowly, with great care, they floated her into deeper water until the stretcher could be pulled away. The onlookers, including hundreds of holidaymakers, cheered in excitement. Some had come to see a show at the dolphinarium but were treated to a much more important spectacle: the life-and-death struggle of a stranded dolphin. Lumpy was swimming in a straight line out to sea towards Mr. Sperm, about a quarter of a mile away. The rescuers knew they had to keep a vigilant watch for hours to prevent Lumpy from stranding again on the beach.

Mr. Sperm was overwhelmed with emotion when he saw Lumpy swim back to him.

"Mr. Sperm, I believe you are crying," Lumpy remarked.

Mr. Sperm, at first, denied it but then admitted, "Of course not!"

"I was just...," he hesitated.

"...crying," said Lumpy.

They shared a moment of vulnerability.

Lumpy asked, "What are we going to do now?"

Mr. Sperm replied, "We'll wait here for now."

***

MDC and BDMLR sprang into action, issuing press releases to inform the world about Lumpy's rescue and the efforts of the dedicated volunteers who had saved her life.

"A bottlenose dolphin that was stranded outside Morecambe Dolphin was successfully refloated back into the Irish Sea by divers from British Marine Life Rescue. Initially, campaigners from the Morecambe Dolphin Campaign attended and did a great job in establishing the dolphin's condition before our members arrived. Our vet examined the young female and noted a slight deformity in the caudal fluke, along with some unknown lumps on her body. Skin samples have been taken for analysis. We will stay on-site for the coming hours to ensure there is no re-stranding. There are several hundreds of strandings each year around the UK coastline. We run courses that instruct members of the public on what they can do in such incidents, and, as a voluntary organisation, we welcome donations."

Lumpy's story of survival and the efforts of those who rescued her served as a reminder of the importance of protecting marine life and the dedication of those who work tirelessly to ensure their well-being.

MDC

Members of our group noticed a young stranded bottlenose dolphin close to the dolphinarium. Currently, the dolphinarium holds Rocky, a male dolphin, and "Happy," a female dolphin.

We immediately alerted the coastguard and police, who in turn contacted the British Divers Marine Life Rescue (BDMLR), and they responded swiftly. Before their arrival, we took necessary measures, including placing cushions under the stranded dolphin and cooling her with seawater to prevent dehydration.

As we send out this information, we can confirm that the stranded dolphin is a young female who has rejoined a Sperm Whale about 400 meters from the shore.

Happy, as Morecambe dolphinarium calls her, joined Rocky earlier this year. Rocky's previous companion, Lady, had tragically passed away, and there have been claims that Rocky may have played a role in her demise. New legislation set to take effect in August 1993 specifies that only mixed-gender dolphin displays can continue, which may explain why they acquired Happy, ensuring the dolphinarium's continued operation.

Based on our research, we believe that Happy was captured in the Mediterranean earlier this year, and astonishingly, Lumpy is her daughter. DNA from skin samples has confirmed this remarkable connection. What boggles the mind is how a Sperm Whale and a juvenile dolphin managed to locate her mother in the Morecambe dolphinarium and travel hundreds of miles to be reunited.

We are calling upon the Department of the Environment to intervene and remove a dolphin named Happy from the dolphinarium and return her to the sea to be reunited with her daughter, a dolphin we affectionately refer to as Lumpy due to unusual markings on her body.

We are also urging the British public to boycott dolphin shows. Our campaign has already succeeded in convincing the local council to cease promoting this outdated form of animal entertainment, as they have removed it from their tourism brochures. In 1990, there were only four dolphinariums in the UK, located here, at Flamingo Land, Brighton, and Windsor. It's high time we say, "Thanks, but no tanks," and make the UK dolphinarium-free!

When the media received our press releases, they made headlines on the front pages. The press knew what sold papers and headlines like "Make Happy *happy* again." "Let her swim free with her daughter" resonated with the public.

Suddenly, MDC found friends in prominent publications, such as the Mail on Sunday, which encouraged its readers to support an "Into the Blue" campaign. Major organisations also saw an opportunity to support a good cause and gain positive media coverage, offering their expertise to complement grassroots efforts. These organisations proposed a plan to fly three dolphins – Rocky, Misse, and Silver – from Brighton to the Turks and Caicos Isles in the British West Indies. There, they would undergo extensive rehabilitation in an 80-acre enclosed sea area, experiencing ocean currents and learning to catch live fish again after years of performing tricks for humans in exchange for dead fish bits with added vitamins.

Happy and Lumpy had spent less time in captivity, so their transition would be simpler. An area outside the dolphinarium would be enclosed for observation.

The defenders of the captive dolphin industry predictably opposed the idea, claiming that these dolphins wouldn't survive in the wild, suggesting that it was better for them to stay in human "care" and continue to generate profits for the industry. However, the movement was gaining momentum.

While nothing happened immediately, people stopped paying to enter the dolphinarium. Instead, crowds gathered on the beach to witness the unique bond between Mr. Sperm and Lumpy. Occasionally, Lumpy would jump or breach, and onlookers would scramble to capture the breathtaking spectacle on film while others observed in awe at this natural display of wildlife.

Lumpy said to Mr. Sperm, "It's my way of saying thanks to the humans who helped me."

Mr. Sperm replied, "It's a remarkable display of your gratitude, Lumpy." He was gratified to see the humans' concern for her.

The owner of the Morecambe dolphinarium soon realised that his business was dwindling. If he couldn't meet the new standards that would come into effect in August 1993, he would likely be forced to shut down. As a savvy businessman, he recognised that it was more prudent to capitalise on the prevailing public sentiment and donate the dolphins to the "Into the Blue" program.

Events progressed swiftly. Fearing the loss of his star performers and his job, the dolphinarium's trainer relocated Rocky to another dolphinarium in Yorkshire, Flamingo Land, under the pretext that the heating in the pool had failed. Flamingo Land was more than willing to take in a male dolphin, hoping Rocky might serve as a stud for their three female dolphins, Betty, Lotty, and Sharky, and help them comply with the forthcoming legislation.

Another press conference was convened, where experts outlined the program for Lumpy and Happy, formerly known as Grumpy.

Doug, who had worked in the industry, provided insight. "We plan to fence off around 80 acres of a sea pen area adjacent to the dolphinarium and place 'Happy and Lumpy' in this contained area. Vets and other experts will monitor their health, and once we're confident they are well, we will remove the pen." Doug continued, "We believe these two dolphins are a mother and daughter originating from the Mediterranean Sea. The mother was captured there, and the daughter swam all the way here with a sperm whale – the same whale you currently see offshore. It's an unprecedented scientific phenomenon."

Many recorded sightings on their journey indicated that the daughter had, indeed, been partially riding on the back of the whale. As a result, the sea pen area was constructed by members of the British Marine Life Rescue Divers, who then placed Happy on one of their stretchers and gently lifted her from the pool to the sea pen.

All the while, Mr. Sperm and Lumpy watched with great interest and curiosity. Lumpy, in particular, swam close to the divers, recognising some of them from her rescue on the beach.

Excitement filled the air as Lumpy and Happy were released into the sea pen. It was a heartwarming sight as the two dolphins swam toward each other, and the divers opened the gate to allow them to reunite. Their meeting was akin to a human mother and daughter embracing after fearing they would never see each other again. Tears of joy flowed, and they leapt for joy as they communicated with one another.

Lumpy asked her mother, "What happened, Mum?"

Happy began to recount her journey, "Well, after I saw those wicked men toss you back into the sea, I was taken to a bigger boat, and it brought me here. I found myself in a small tank with a male dolphin; I think he was called Rocky. It seems he had been there for some years."

Lumpy interrupted, "And what are those marks on your body?"

Happy explained, "Those are teeth marks; Rocky would rake his teeth if I told him to leave me alone." She went on to describe how Rocky had been trained to perform tricks for humans, jumping through a hoop and swimming vertically on his fluke tail. "If he did these tricks well, the trainer would reward him with titbits of dead fish while the humans clapped. I didn't eat for a day, but I became hungry and ate, although it was disgusting. Swimming around that tank day after day was incredibly boring. I didn't think I could survive in there for long."

Lumpy empathised with her mother, and she asked, "How did you find me, my dear daughter?"

Lumpy shared her incredible journey, "After I was left alone, I found Mr. Sperm whale. He said he would help me find you. We discovered that you were here, and we swam for several days. I rode on the back of this great leviathan – I love him, Mum."

Reflecting on the males of their kind, Happy muttered, "Hmm, perhaps there are some good males in these seas."

Lumpy added, "We had great adventures. He saved some humans who were drifting in a small boat by pushing them to shore. We nearly got snared in fishing nets, too. On our journey, we saw many humans waving to us from the shore, and even boats came close to take photographs. When we reached the place called Morecambe dolphinarium, I swam toward it and got stuck on the shore, but some kind of humans rescued me."

Grumpy, once again begrudgingly, muttered, "Maybe there are some good humans after all."

Lumpy and Grumpy spent several weeks in the sea pen, during which they were fed a variety of live fish, and underwater cameras were installed to ensure they could catch live fish for themselves. While they acclimated, Mr. Sperm would occasionally leave for hours or even a day, needing to swim great distances to catch the quantity of fish required for sustenance.

Eventually, the guardians overseeing the dolphins were satisfied with their health and deemed them ready to be released from the pen into the Irish Sea. Boats would follow them as closely as possible, but they had a significant advantage – the sight of a massive sperm whale.

Upon their release, a crowd had gathered to witness the sea pen net being lifted. The spectators clapped, and the divers bid the dolphins a bon voyage as they swam to reunite with Mr. Sperm.

As they swam together, Lumpy asked, "Where are we going?" The other two replied in unison, "Home." Lumpy had grown stronger by some miracle or perhaps due to finding her mother, and her movements through the sea were becoming more effortless. Thus, she needed less time riding on the whale's back, although for a brief moment, in a playful jest, Lumpy hopped on the whale's back. Her time in captivity had weakened her both physically and mentally.

Their journey south was monitored by boats, and large groups of humans were drawn to catch a glimpse of the cetaceans.

Mr. Sperm maintained his assertion that it was because they believed he was truly great, to which Lumpy and Grumpy playfully responded, "It's because of your big head."

In due time, they arrived in the Mediterranean Sea, their home waters. A pod of common dolphins spotted them and wondered aloud, "Is that Lumpy and her mother?" Others were sceptical, thinking, "No, it can't be – they must be dead."

Lumpy interjected, "You're both wrong; we're very much alive."

The commons were astonished and peppered Lumpy and Grumpy with questions. "Where have you been? What happened?"

Lumpy replied, "We've been on an adventure, but if you want to know the whole story, it's going to cost you ten squids for Mr. Sperm's stomach!"

Mr. Sperm chimed in, sharing the news of their successful mission and the release of a dolphin known as Rocky, along with two others from a different dolphinarium in Brighton. He added that there were now only a few captive comrades left in England, at Flamingo Land and Windsor. He had heard that human friends were campaigning to have their comrades freed, as these dolphins were born to be free and should return to the open sea.

As he spoke, other dolphins gathered to listen, and finally, he said, "I want you to consider this: if we are to survive the human onslaught on us, I suggest we need to interact with them. Perhaps the whales should gather in areas of the sea where humans can watch us; they can call it whale watching, and some dolphins can interact with them either in pods or as solitary dolphins. This engagement may be the key to our survival by showing them in our environment we are as good as them," he paused and, true to his big-headed nature, said, "better!"

All the assembled dolphins cheered, "Here, here, freedom, freedom, life and freedom."

Grumpy spoke, "We are in your debt, Mr. Sperm. For so many years, I dismissed males for their uncaring attitudes towards females, but having you as a dear friend to my daughter and freedom fighter, I realise now not to judge all males as the same."

As her mother spoke, Lumpy began to cry. Mr. Sperm said, "It was a great honour to fight for your freedom. It shows the greatness of our cetacean nation, a whale fighting for a dolphin's liberty. Now, I must embark on another mission. My mother has sent me a voice message. She has a problem with her liaison with one of those enchanting singers, Mr. Humpback. I told her nothing good would come from a Sperm female living with a Humpback male, but she fell head over flippers in love with him. Personally, I think they were not cute or handsome like me…"

Before he finished, Lumpy inquired, "When will we see you again?" Correcting herself, she asked, "Or when will we hear from you again? I will miss your big head and riding on your back, but I won't miss those 'things' – referring to the lice and barnacles. Please take care of yourself on your journey."

He bid farewell to Lumpy and Grumpy, and the assembled dolphins formed a line of honour as he embarked on his long journey to the South Atlantic. Lumpy and Grumpy swam with him for a short distance, and as they parted ways, he remarked, "Next time I see you, I want those ten squids you owe me." With a resounding laugh, he disappeared into the vast ocean, leaving Lumpy and Grumpy to continue their journey of freedom.

Humans, because their flaws, are losing
their connection to the ocean and nature
a bond vital for their survival.
By bridging the gap between sea and land,
dolphins can inspire humans to change,
reminding them of the beauty, balance,
and wisdom found in the ocean.
Mr. Sperm calls upon the dolphins to guide
humanity back to harmony, before it's too late.
South Atlantic

Not Quite The End

Among the group of dolphins who had gathered to hear Mr. Sperm's speech was a dolphin named Freddy. He had been utterly captivated by the tales of adventure and yearned for something more than the routine life of tides, fish, and more tides. Turning to his fellow dolphins, he expressed his desire, "I'm fed up with this everyday life. The tides come in, the tides go out, fish swim by, and well, fish swim by again. I want to experience life and have fun, and I need a holiday. I want to be an ambassador for our dolphins."

And so it happened that a wild solitary dolphin made his way to a place called Amble in the north of England. Many humans flocked to this location to catch a glimpse of Freddy, and for many of them, he became the best friend they'd ever had. They cherished him like a beloved family "pet." But Freddy was no pet, and when the time came for him to move on, his mission fulfilled, many had come to realise that a wild dolphin had unconditionally welcomed them into his life. One person profoundly touched by this experience was the author.

Freddy's parting message to his admirers and all of humanity was a plea: "SAVE THE DOLPHINS." In his characteristic, mischievous style, he added, "THANKS FOR ALL THE FISH, AMBLE."

Orgs to contact

MARINE

Sea Shepherd - direct anti-whaling

European Cetacean Bycatch Campaign

Marine Conservation

British Diver Marine Life Rescue

MIGRATION

Freedom From Torture

CHILD HELP

UNICEF - United Nations

Toybox - street children

Sponsorship-SOS Children Villages

Compassion

World Vision

Alan Cooper

The End